snow

To Tijana, Milica, and Stefan—my very special friends.
And very special thanks to Helen Mortimer, my editor.
—M.S.

THIS IS A BORZOI BOOK PUBLISHED BY
ALFRED A. KNOPF

Copyright © 2002 by Manya Stojic

All rights reserved under International and Pan-American Copyright Conventions.
Published in the United States of America by Alfred A. Knopf, a division of
Random House, Inc., New York,
and simultaneously in Canada by Random House of Canada Limited, Toronto. Distributed by
Random House, Inc., New York. Published in the United Kingdom by David Bennett Books
Limited, an imprint of Chrysalis Books, plc.
KNOPF, BORZOI BOOKS, and the colophon are registered trademarks of Random House, Inc.

www.randomhouse.com/kids
Library of Congress Cataloging-in-Publication Data
Stojic, Manya.
Snow/Manya Stojic.—1st ed.
p. cm.
Summary: As snow approaches and begins to fall, Moose, Bear, Fox, and other forest
creatures prepare for winter.
ISBN 0-375-82348-4 — ISBN 0-375-92348-9 (lib. bdg.)
[1. Forest animals—Fiction. 2. Snow—Fiction. 3. Winter—Fiction.] I. Title.
PZ7.S873 Sn 2002
[E]—dc21 2002066146

Printed in Hong Kong
November 2002
10 9 8 7 6 5 4 3 2 1
First American Edition

snow
Manya Stojic

Alfred A. Knopf 🐎 New York

$\bigcirc$wl ruffled
her feathers.
"The **snow** is coming,"
she said wisely.
"I know snow."

The geese
were gathering.

"S-S-S-SNOW?"

they said with a shiver.
"Our lake will
freeze."

"Yes, the snow is coming," said Moose. "I can smell it on the breeze."

"Aaah, snow," Bear yawned. "Time for me to be sleeping."

Hare snuggled her bunnies. "Winter brings snow, my honeys, and our white coats."

"Oh! Snow!" said Fox. "Those clouds are **full of snow.**"

And then it
SNOWED.

White snowflakes
swirled in
the sky.

Some very big.
Some very small.
All very gentle.

The forest was **still**. It was covered with a **sparkling blanket.**

"My fur looks like fire,"
bristled Fox,

"against this white **snow**."

"We are as white as we can be," giggled the bunnies. "White as snow."

"Snow . . . snow . . . so . . . sleepy," mumbled Bear as he drifted into dreams.

"I love the crisp air," sniffed Moose, "just after it snows."

"South!
We'll fly south,"
honked the geese.

"So long, snow."

"The snow will stay," said Owl.

"But one spring day, it will drip drop melt away."

"I know snow," she said wisely. "But I sing spring."